Kind as a Princess

By Catherine J. Manning • Illustrated by Sarah Conradsen

Random House 🏠 New York

rhcbooks.com
ISBN 978-0-7364-4202-2 (trade)
MANUFACTURED IN CHINA
10 9 8 7 6 5 4 3 2 1

Random House Children's Books supports the First Amendment and celebrates the right to read.

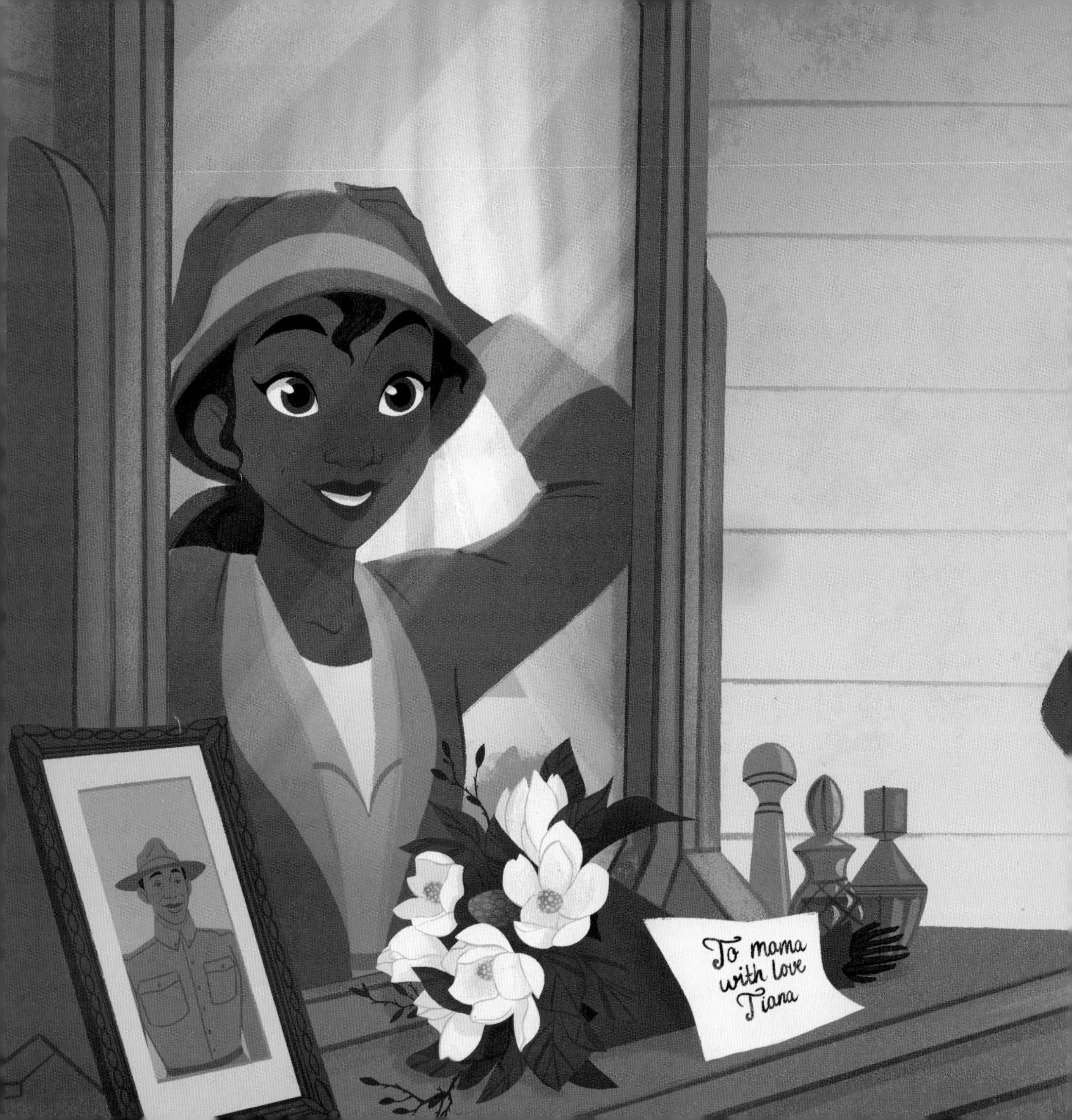
To mama
with love
Tiana

Princesses are kind. But what does that mean?

Kindness

is being brave enough to care—for the world, for others . . . and for you, too!

FRENCH CUISINE

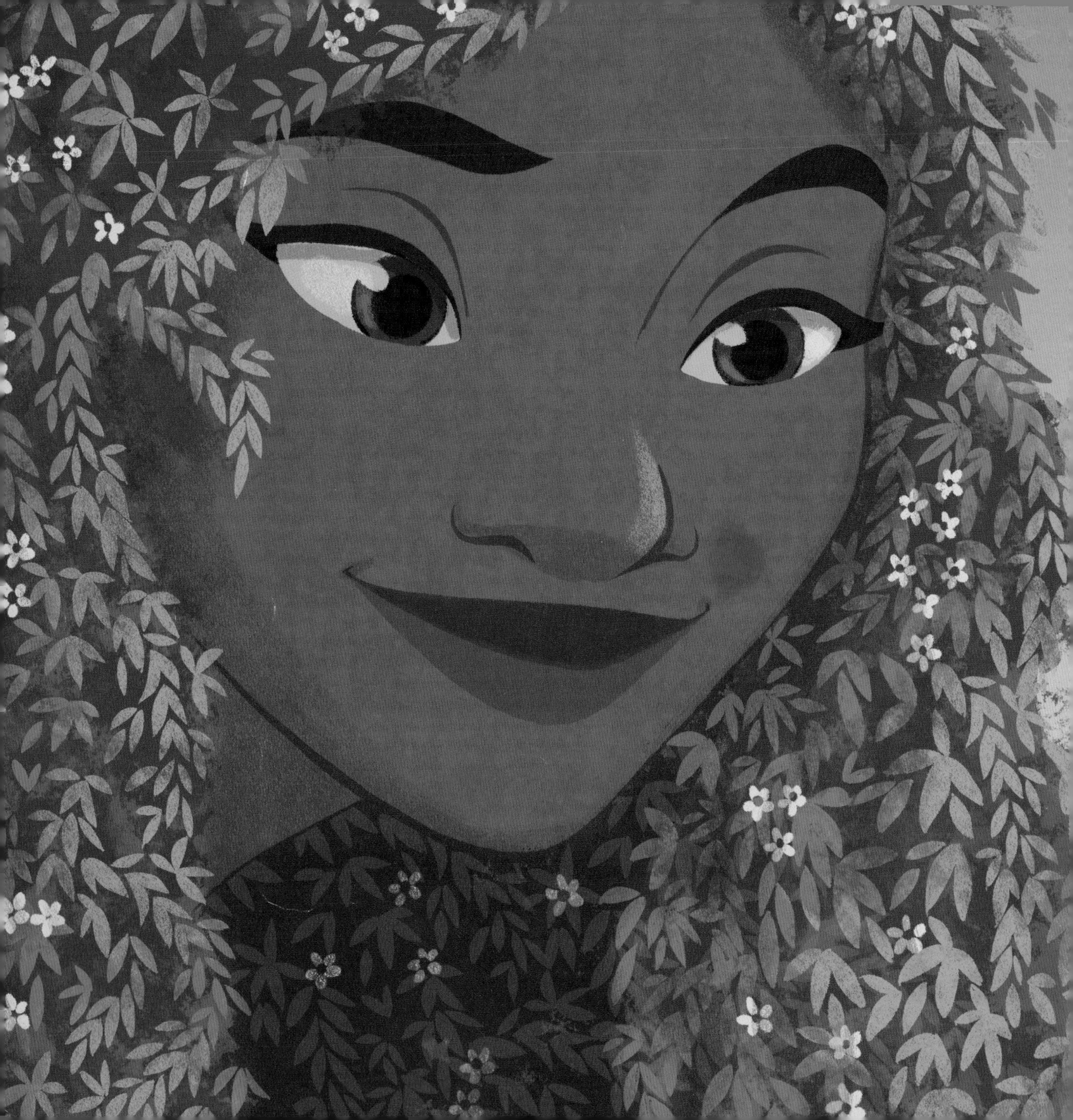

Moana helps others find the

goodness

in their hearts. Her courage helps her see the goodness inside them, too.

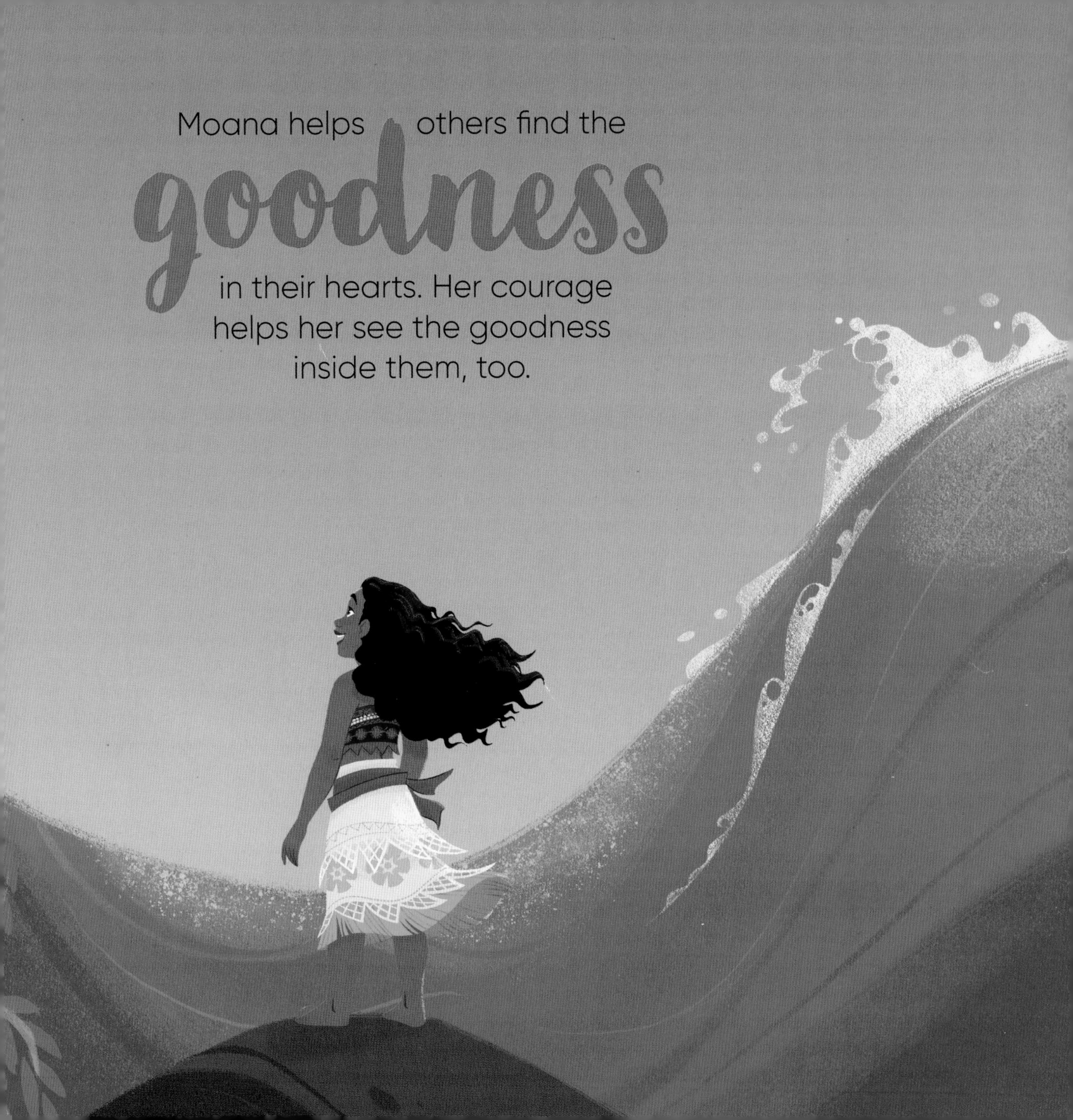

Rapunzel gives
each friend a turn. . . .

Jasmine shows she cares by

sharing.

Belle knows that sometimes **self-kindness** means **standing up** to bullies.

And Snow White knows
how to ask for help.

After all, *help* is a brave, kind gift!

Pocahontas thanks the Earth for the gifts it gives.

She shows she *cares* with gratitude.

Cinderella
lends a hand
whenever she can.

Ariel shows herself *love* and *care* when things get hard.

Merida is sure to say she's **sorry** when she does something **UNKIND**.

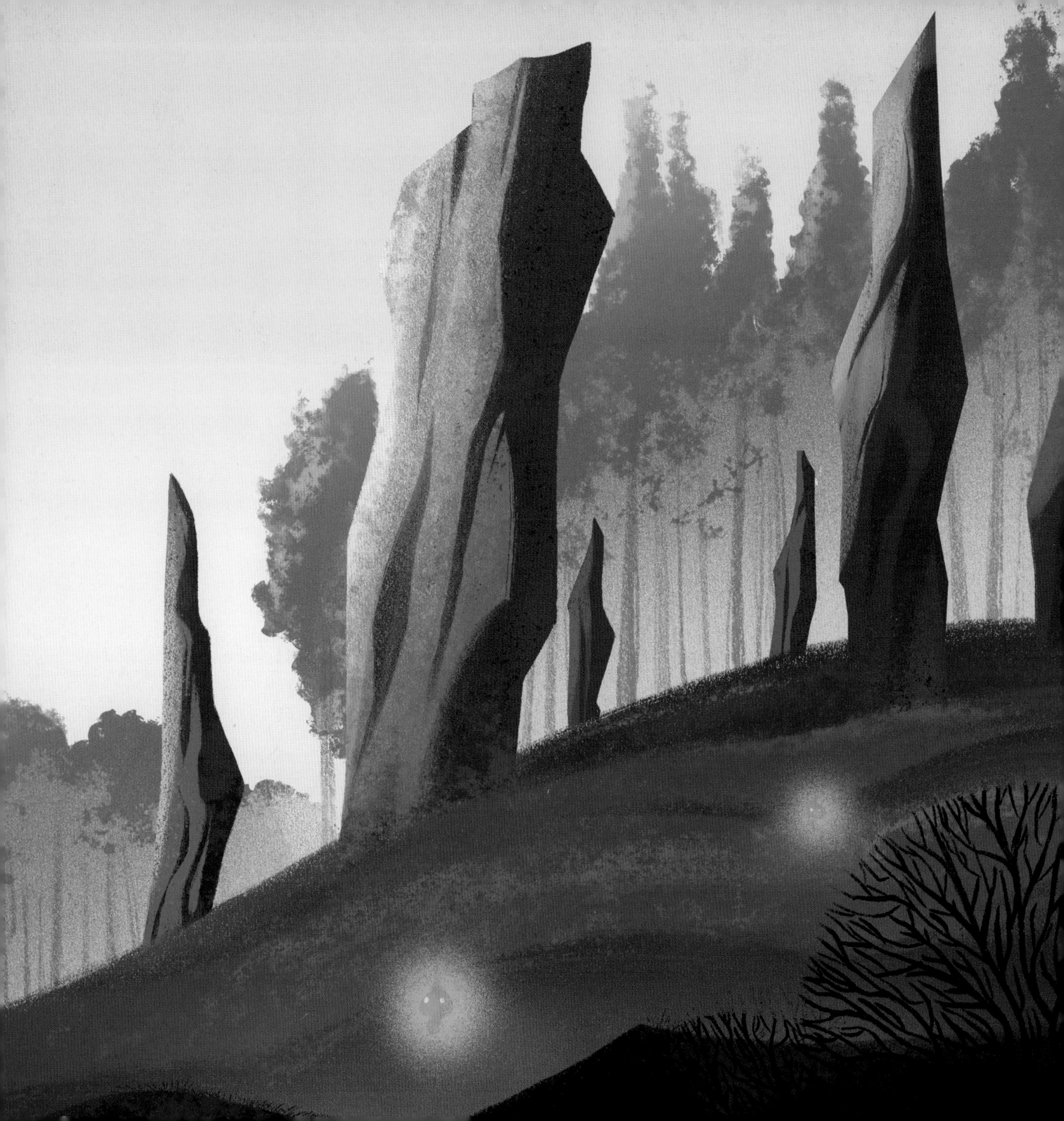

Jasmine respects herself—she uses a
brave voice
to speak her mind!

Aurora respectfully *listens* to others' brave voices, too.

Mulan *cares* for the **WORLD** by doing **what's right**.

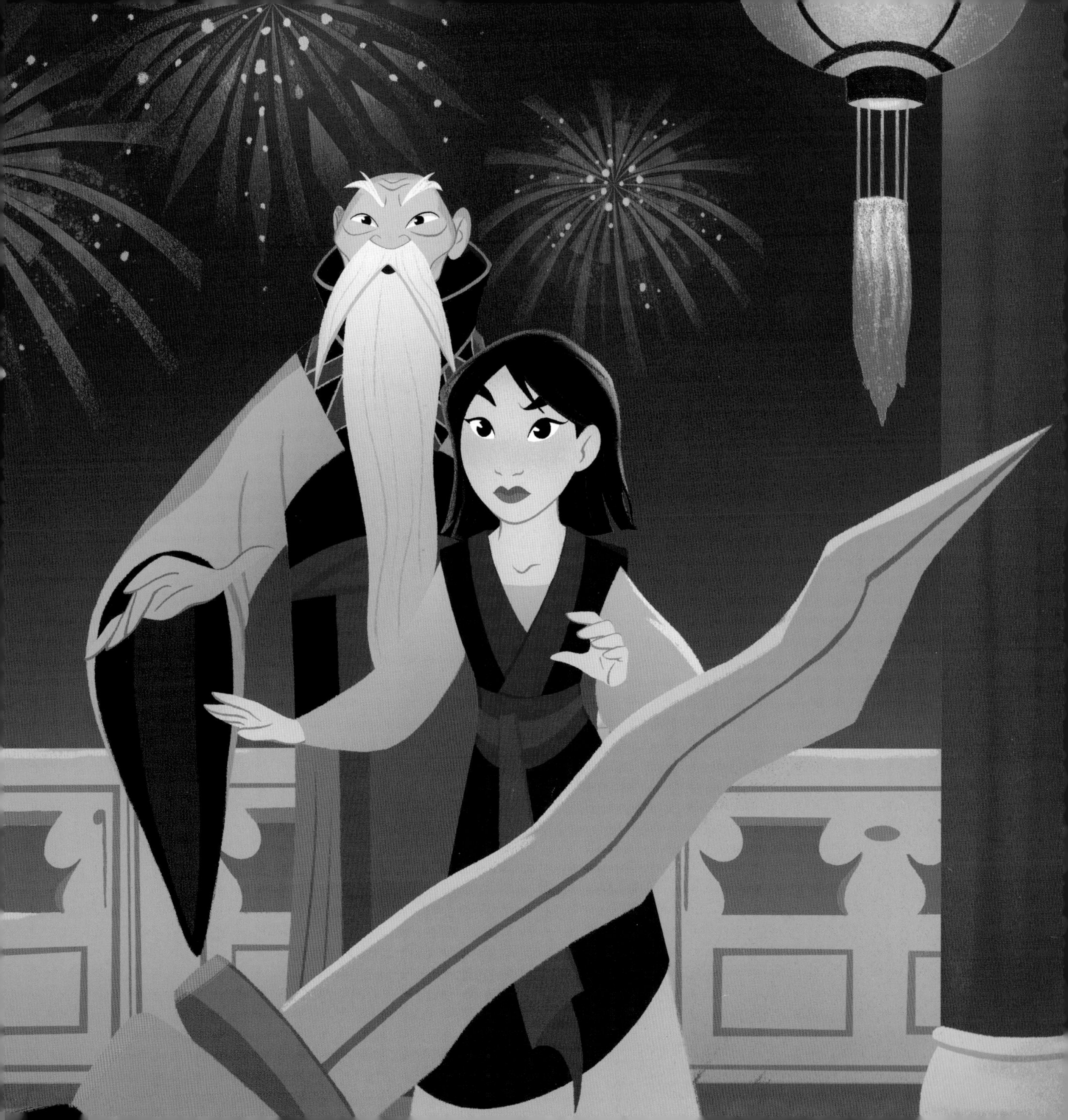

Tiana cares for herself by **working hard** to *follow* her DREAMS.

Rapunzel cheers others on as they *follow their* **dreams**, too.

Ariel says goodbye to her loved ones.

She shows them that she Cares.

You can be as kind as a princess.
Go the extra mile with

love,

respect,

and **care**–

–for yourself and everyone!

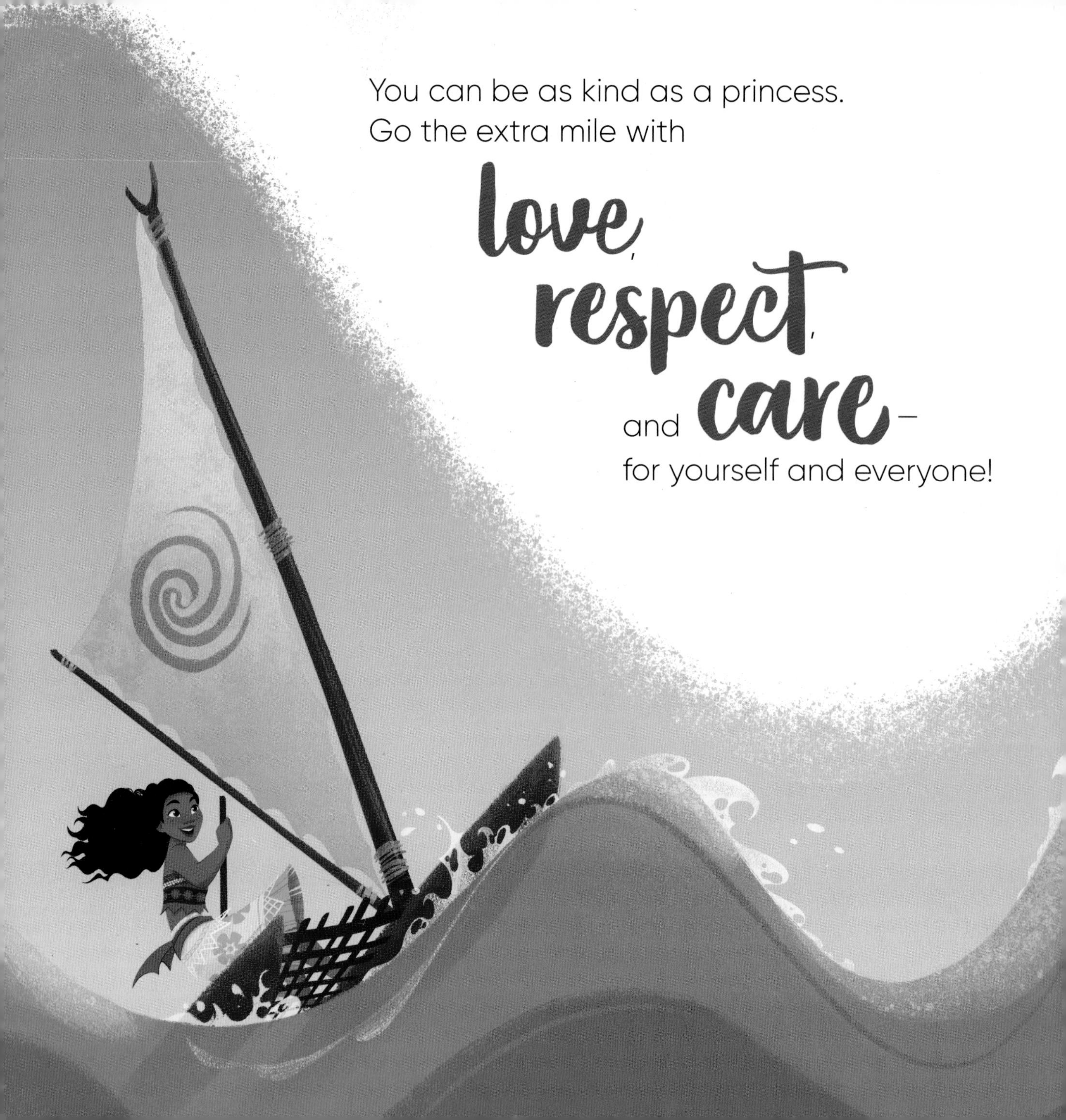